Act Normal And Make Everything Fair
By
Christian Darkin

First printing 2016
Rational Stories
www.RationalStories.com

The illustrations are by the author, but use some elements for which I'd like to credit and thank: www.obsidiandawn.com, kuschelirmel-stock, Theshelfs and waywardgal at Deviantart.com
Story and illustrations by © Christian Darkin

CHAPTER 1

I had decided to do something to give everyone in our town some fun. I wasn't quite sure what, because things that are fun for children often aren't so much fun for grownups, and things that are fun for grownups are often not much fun for children.

I decided to do something that was fair for everyone.

In this story, I do end up getting chased by some ghosts, and locking the Prime Minister in a big wheel. I also nearly ruin the election, but I think it all works out OK in the end.

Oh, and just in case you don't know, The Prime Minister is the person in charge of the whole country, and everything that happens in it. The Prime Minister's only job is to make sure everything is fair, so you would think it would be an easy job.

It turns out that it's not easy at all, and that's why we don't just have one person running the country all the time. Every five years, we all have to pick who we think would be able to do it best, and let them have a go. When we do that, it is called an ELECTION.

People in this story:

Me: I'm Jenny. I like to understand why things happen. Sometimes the best way to understand why things happen is to make something happen and then watch what happens next. What happens next is usually an adventure.

Adam: Adam is my little brother. He has really started to like reading, and normally, I would say that was a good thing. But, Adam has a way of making a mess with everything he does, and it turns out that you can make a really big mess with reading. Especially when you don't remember where all the pages go.

Dad: When my brother and I argue, Dad has lots of ways to get us to agree, but they usually end up with neither of us getting exactly what we want. I've discovered that this is a bit like the way elections work.

CHAPTER 2

"It's not fair!" Adam said to Dad.

I don't remember exactly how the argument started. I remember that Dad wanted to go to the market to buy some dragon fruit for a recipe he was going to try out on us.

I wanted to stay at home and build a rocket, and Adam wanted to see how many glasses he could knock over with a football.

Anyway, Dad said we should take a vote (that's when everyone puts their hand up for their favourite idea, and whoever gets the most hands wins).

Dad also said Adam's idea couldn't be in the vote, because too many things would get broken. He also said that if we didn't go to the market, he couldn't make our tea, so in the end, Dad's idea got all the votes, and we went to the market.

While Dad was looking for dragon fruit, Adam and I looked for a way to make the town fun for everyone. We soon found it.

Next to the market, there's a poster for a fair. 'FAIR!' it says, and underneath is a picture of a roller-coaster with lots of kids on it having fun. Underneath are the dates when the fair is on, and guess what? It's five years ago! Five years! My brother sees it every time we are in town, and asks if we can go to the fair - and we can't because he would only be a baby and we'd need a time machine. (We don't have a time machine, but I have got some ideas about that which I will try out in another story one day).

But, this time, the poster was covered over by another poster. Not a poster for a fair, but a poster of the Prime Minister.

On top of that was another poster of a lady who wanted to be the Prime Minister but who wasn't.

I knew what this was all about. It was all about the election. (Remember, I said the election is where everyone gets to pick who they think should be the Prime Minister, and when they count up, whoever gets the most votes gets to have a go).

There were only 2 more days to go before the election, so EVERYONE was talking about it. They even did a TV show where all the people who wanted to be Prime Minister stood in a row and argued with each other.

Dad let us stay up and watch it, but I thought they were all very rude and shouty.

Things grow-nups say about the election:

- 'It doesn't matter who wins'
- 'They're all as bad as each other'

- 'All they do is argue'
- 'I'd like to lock them in a room together until they sort it all out' (Grandma says that a lot)

Things I don't understand:

- If all the prime minister has to do is make sure things are fair, why are so many things not fair?

- If it doesn't matter who wins, why is everyone going on about it?

CHAPTER 3

while I was thinking this, Adam was doing some reading. He was reading the bit of the fair poster that he could still see underneath the other posters.

"IF YOU WANT THE FAIR TO COME TO YOUR TOWN, EMAIL US," he was saying. Adam is getting very good at reading.

That was when I had half an idea.

"we should do that," I said, "having a fair will be just the kind of thing to give the children in the town some fun."

Adam thought it was a very good idea, but there were two problems:

- The email address for the fair was covered over by the picture of the Prime Minister.
- A lot of grown-ups don't think fairs are fun, so I would need another half an idea for them.

We went to find Dad.

Dad was not buying dragon fruit. There is a special stall in the market that sells things most kids in my school don't eat. It sells mooli and prickly pears and plantains and goji berries and tamarind and scotch bonnet chillies (which Dad says you can't eat because they will blow your head clean off). I think the woman who runs the stall could be an alien.

But the stall was not there. Instead, there was another stall where another lady who was tall and pointy and could have been a different sort of alien was asking Dad questions about the election. She was writing down the answers on a piece of paper stuck to her clipboard.

"Who are you going to vote for?" The lady asked Dad.

Dad said, "I don't know," and she wrote it down.

I said, "Why write down when someone doesn't know the answer? At school, if I don't know the answer, I don't write, 'I don't know,' I write a guess, or I leave it blank to answer later."

"We're trying to work out who's going to win," she said. "It's called a poll."

"That's silly," I said. "Why not just wait and see?" Behind her, I could see Adam practising writing 'I don't know,' over and over again on some of the lady's other pieces of paper.

Dad said, "Getting people to vote for you is very tiring because there are 60 million people in the country, and talking to all of them takes ages — especially if you have to get them to do something like vote. Anyway, in most towns, everyone votes for the same person, so the important towns are the ones where people don't know."

I said, "What happens if our town doesn't know?"

Dad said, "The people who want to be Prime Minister will all rush here, and there will be a media circus."

That was when I had the other half of my idea. If I had known that a media circus is not like a real circus, I would probably have tried to have a different idea...

When we got home, I told my brother about my two-part idea. While Dad was making tomato pasta (because the dragon-fruit lady was the wrong kind of alien), we wrote an email to all our friends:

Dear everyone,

Please email the fair (I will put the fair's address at the bottom of this email), and ask them to come to our town. If they get enough emails, we will get a fair.

PS: If a lady with a sheet of paper asks your parents who they're going to vote for, tell them to say, 'I don't know.' If they get enough, 'I don't knows,' then our town will be one of the important ones, and we will get a media circus too.

Love, Jenny.

Then, I looked for the fair's email on the Internet, but I couldn't remember the name of the fair on the poster. I should have been able to remember because we'd walked past the poster every day for years and years.

Anyway, Adam couldn't remember either, so we found a list of fairs (there were about

100), and put all the emails on the end of our message, just in case.

It turned out that this was probably a very bad idea, and the next day we found out why....

CHAPTER 4

The first fair turned up very early the next morning. It came in about twenty big lorries, all painted different colours, and it started unpacking on the green in the middle of town.

Fairs are like big Lego. They come as kits which have to be put together in a very special way using instructions. They're a bit like the instructions in Lego boxes only much more complicated.

Adam and I are very interested in the way things get put together, so we went down to watch. The bits of a fair aren't exactly like the bits of a Lego set because instead of blocks and bricks, they have tracks and poles and carts with wheels and boards with giant ghost paintings on. They also have lots and lots of lights.

While the people started putting the pieces together with their big instructions, I asked them lots of questions - especially about the lights, because having so many lights must be bad for global warming which is a Big Problem.

While I was doing that, another two fairs arrived.

The green was getting full of lorries now. There were also lots of bits of fair and more tracks and roller-coaster bits than I have ever seen. There were bits for three ghost trains and enough candy floss machines to make a pink cloud around the whole school.

I could see what had happened. My friends had all emailed ALL of the fairs on the list - and there were about a hundred of them. Now, all the fairs in the country were coming to our town!

More lorries, and more fairs were arriving all the time. I decided that part 1 of my idea was going very well, but the people in charge were all starting to ask a lot of questions.

I decided to just Act Normal, and I went off to try to find Adam.

Adam was sitting on his own behind one of the lorries, quietly doing some reading. I was surprised, because I thought he would be climbing on something, or jumping on something.

Then I saw what he was reading. Adam had collected together all the plans from all the fairs, showing how the rides needed to be put together. The plans were all covered in complicated looking drawings and tiny writing and they were all in a big pile.

Adam was learning how to build a fair, which I thought was a good thing for him to learn, but I also thought that the people building the fairs would probably like their plans back.

I said, "I think the people building the fairs would probably like their plans back."

Adam said, "I might have got them all a bit mixed up."

We decided not to worry too much about that, and we just made the instructions into a few piles. Then, we put each pile where one of the people making the fairs could find it. Then we Acted Normal again, and went home.

The next morning, we found out that this was probably another bad idea...

CHAPTER 5

It was Monday, and so we went out to catch the bus to school. I was carrying a heavy school bag because I had been doing some experiments with electricity and I had decided to take my extra-big battery in for "show and tell".

The problem with catching the bus was that there wasn't a bus at the bus stop. Instead, there was a roller-coaster.

I could see what had happened. The fairs each had a roller-coaster, but when Adam had got their plans mixed up, the fairs must have used ALL the bits, and made one big roller-coaster all around the town.

This sounded like a lot of fun.

We got on the roller-coaster, and it started rolling along our road. It turned left, then right, then it went up and over one of the houses, and did a big loop. It got faster and faster and faster, swooping up and down and round the buildings and streets.

It wound around the big clock tower, and got higher and higher. When I looked down, I could see that it wasn't just the roller-coaster. The whole town was covered in fairs. There were dodgems and waltzers and stalls, and there were flashing lights EVERYWHERE!

where the three big roundabouts were, there were now three of those bumpy round rides with teacups on them. The teacups were going round and round each other in a big swirl like a traffic jam, but with giant tea cups.

The whole of the shopping centre had been turned into a ghost train, and people were going in to do their shopping and then running out again, screaming.

The town looked like a lot more fun than it had been yesterday, so I thought things were going well.

Some of the grown-ups didn't look very happy because the roads were full of roller-coasters and giant tea cups, and because there were ghosts and skeletons in the shopping centre. I thought that was OK, because the grown-ups would be happy once the media circus arrived.

Our roller-coaster zoomed on until it got to the school, but it didn't stop. It went straight past, and on, up the road until it got to the end of town where it ran out of track.

I could see that it was about to start rolling back into town, so we hopped off.

That was when we met the Prime Minister.

He looked just like he did in the picture, only a lot more tired, because he had spent weeks and weeks going from one town to the next, telling people to vote for him.

This was part 2 of my idea starting to work.

Everybody had told their parents to say, "I don't know," when anyone asked who they were going to vote for.

That meant that the Prime Minister had come to our town to tell everyone to vote for him. He was even holding a speech to read to everyone.

I couldn't see a circus with him, but he was running towards us and there were A LOT of people chasing him.

They were holding cameras and microphones, and they were all shouting questions at him.

"What are you doing here?

What is that roller-coaster for?

why is the town full of ghosts and skeletons?

Is it your fault?"

The Prime Minister tripped over Adam and let go of his speech. Suddenly, all the people with cameras started photographing us, and shouting questions at us as well.

Adam thought it would be fun to shout questions back at them, and they flashed and shouted even more. Adam laughed, but it was very difficult to think about anything with all that noise going on. Then he picked up the Prime Minister's speech and ran after him.

I didn't know exactly what was going on, but I thought that, if the Prime Minister was running away, we should probably run away too.

Adam is very fast, so he ran past the Prime Minister. He jumped into the front of the roller-coaster, just as it started rolling away.

We jumped into the middle of the train and started climbing forward over the seats. We were getting faster and faster.

When I looked behind me, all the people with cameras had jumped into the back of the roller-coaster, shouting and clicking their cameras.

"Who are they?" I asked the Prime Minister.

He said, "They all work for the newspapers and the TV," and then he told me that, because news often happens around the Prime Minister, they all follow him around ALL THE TIME, trying to be first to find things out.

"Why don't you just tell them the news?" I asked.

He said, "I do, but when I got here, I didn't know how to get into town because of all the fairground rides."

"So?" I said. "Why not just tell them that?"

"Because," said the Prime Minister, "I'm the Prime Minister, so I'm supposed to know everything. If I don't know something, I have to just Act Normal and pretend that I do, or people will think I'm not a very good Prime Minister."

"So, you have to run away every time you don't know something?" I said.

"Yes," said the Prime Minister.

I said, "I have to Act Normal a lot as well. It's very tiring."

The roller-coaster raced into town, zooming up and down and round in circles, around roads and houses, and all the rides and duck-hooking stalls and hot-dog stands that had been put up all over the town.

I asked the Prime Minister, "Is it like this all the time for you?"

He said, "A bit, yes."

I said, "Good, because I thought it was just me that this sort of thing happened to."

Adam was enjoying the ride and trying to read the Prime Minister's speech at the same time. Every time we went up a hill, all the papers got mixed up, and every time we went down a hill, they got stuck to Adam's face.

The Prime Minister was looking worried, so I thought I'd ask him some of my questions.

"Why don't you just make everything fair?" I said. "Then everyone would vote for you."

He pulled a funny face and screamed. (I think that was because we were going downhill very fast). Then, he started telling me a big list of things he had done, but I couldn't hear what he was saying because a helter-skelter had started playing "Gangnam Style" very loudly as we went past.

In the end, the roller-coaster rolled slowly to a stop, and I was just thinking of another question to ask, when things started to get really bad...

CHAPTER 6

The news people started climbing out of the roller-coaster and running up towards us.

I grabbed the Prime Minister with one hand, and Adam with the other, and we ran!

We climbed onto a merry-go-round, but we had to run in between the horses and the dragons. That took us round in a circle, and we had to dodge behind a candy-floss stall.

I tried making beards out of candy-floss to disguise us.

It didn't work. The news people were still following. While we were trying to get our candy-floss beards off, we crashed straight into a lady in a suit.

I recognised her right away. She was the lady who's face was on the OTHER poster we had seen. She was the lady who wanted to be Prime Minister instead of the Prime Minister we had already got with us.

She was also holding a speech, and she was also being followed by another, even bigger, crowd of news people.

She had a "Battle Bus". (I knew that's what it was because it said, "Battle Bus" on the side and had a big picture of her smiling on it). The Battle Bus was her way of getting from place to place, so that she could tell people to vote for her, but it wasn't doing any battling, because it was stuck between a "hall of mirrors" and a hot-dog stand.

All the news people following the Prime Minister saw all the news people following the lady who wanted to be Prime Minister. Then ALL the news people saw me and Adam, and the Prime Minister, AND the lady who wanted to be Prime Minister, all together.

They all decided that some important news must be about to happen.

They all started shouting, and flashing their cameras, and climbing over rides to get to us.

I grabbed the lady who wanted to be Prime Minister, and said, "If you don't know what's going on, you'd better come with us!"

She came with us, and we all started running together.

When I looked back, I could see hundreds and hundreds of news people. Some were hanging onto the Battle Bus. Some were tripping over each other's cameras. Some were getting covered in candy floss and rubber ducks and hot-dogs. Some were getting confused by the hall of mirrors and crashing into each other.

It was very funny and they reminded me of a lot of clowns. I decided that this was what people meant by a media circus.

The news people were faster at running than us. I think it's because they run after people all the time, so they're used to it —and they don't have big shoes like real clowns. But I had a good idea of how to escape.

I pulled Adam, and the lady who wanted to be Prime Minister, and the man who was already Prime Minister onto a dodgem car.

The Prime Minister and the lady had to hold onto the sides because I put Adam into the driving seat. (which was probably a bad idea).

Dodgems use electricity so they have a metal pole on top, and they only go when electricity from the roof goes down the pole. But instead, I took out my extra-big battery. (Remember, I had an extra-big battery in my school bag for "show and tell").

I attached the battery onto the top of the dodgem and we went zooming off down the street. We had to hold on very tight because my brother isn't very good at steering, or NOT crashing into things.

He is very good at going fast, though, and he zig-zagged down the street, with all the people with cameras running after us.

I told him to steer us into the shopping centre to try to hide. The floor of the shopping centre was very flat, so we managed to go very fast past all the shops.

I tried asking the lady who wanted to be Prime Minister why she thought she would be better at it than the man who already was Prime Minister.

"I believe in schools," she said.

I said, "That's silly. Everyone believes in schools – you just need to look and you can see them. You don't get to decide if you believe in them. They're not like ghosts."

She was about to say something, then she changed her mind and instead, said, "I can see ghosts!"

She pointed behind us, and she was right because as well as the people with cameras, we were also now being chased by some skeletons, three monsters, and a ghost.

Do you remember why?

CHAPTER 7

It was because the shopping centre had been turned into a giant ghost train.

"They're not real ghosts," said the Prime Minister.

"I knew that," said the lady who wanted to be Prime Minister.

"I bet you didn't!" said the Prime Minister.

Then they started arguing. First, they were arguing about ghosts, but then, they started arguing about people dressed as ghosts and how dressing as a ghost in a ghost train wasn't a very good job. (It sounded like a good job to me.) Then, they started arguing about why people couldn't get good jobs. Then, they started arguing about whether schools helped people to get good jobs.

The Prime Minister said, "There should be bigger schools, with better libraries and more sports stuff!"

I thought that was a really good idea, until the lady who wanted to be Prime Minister said, "No. There should be SMALLER schools, with more teachers, so everyone knows everyone else!" That sounded like a good idea too.

It was interesting, but it might have been better for them to argue about how we were going to get away from all the people chasing us because my giant battery was starting to wear out, and so the dodgem was slowing down, and the ghost had got a lot closer...

My brother zoomed us out of the shopping centre, but I could see a whole group of news people coming down the street. Some were running. Some had motorbikes and some had helicopters.

The other way, the street was blocked by a giant Ferris wheel. It was one of those ones that has big, round, glass rooms all round it. You can stand inside and look out over the town, while it moves round, in a big circle. The people from the fair hadn't completely finished building it yet, because I could see the control box, and the wires connecting it up hadn't been put together.

That was when I had an idea. It was an idea about how we could get away from the news people. It was also an idea about how we could get all the arguing finished with before the election.

It was something Grandma often said that gave me the idea...

CHAPTER 8

...Grandma often said, "I'd like to lock them all in a room together, until they sort it all out!"

I decided we could do that, and escape from the media circus at the same time, so I pointed at the wheel, and my brother drove the dodgem through the door, into the glass room.

Just before the door shut behind us, I jumped off, ran out into the ride's control box, and plugged my battery into the loose wires.

Then, I jumped back in, and we started to move. It was like being in a bubble, and we slowly went up, and up, until the news people were all just little dots, and we couldn't hear their shouting, or see the flashes of their cameras.

My battery was running out, and it wasn't strong enough to make the ride go fast, so just as we got to the top, the whole wheel stopped.

We had escaped.

The Prime Minister, and the lady who wanted to be Prime Minister sat down. They both looked really tired.

"Now," I said to them in my best serious voice. "This has all got a bit silly, hasn't it? I want you to talk about everything, until you both agree."

They both always said they wanted to make things better for everybody, so I didn't think it would take very long for them to agree.

But, it did.

They talked about schools and whether lots of small schools were better, or whether fewer big schools were better. Then, they argued about how much money people had.

The prime minister thought people who worked harder should get more money, and the lady thought that some people were getting far too much, and some weren't getting enough.

Then, they argued about global warming. I know a bit about global warming, and I think it's a Bad Thing, but it turns out both of them think it's a Bad Thing too but they don't agree about what to do.

I was going to tell them my idea of building a new ice-cap, but then I remembered that

I'd tried that at Christmas and it hadn't turned out to be such a good idea. (You can read about that in another story).

It got dark, and they were still arguing, and still getting more and more tired.

Then, suddenly, in the middle of an argument about hospitals, the lady who wanted to be Prime Minister started to cry.

"What's the matter?" said Adam.

But I knew what the matter was. I had seen my brother cry like that before lots of times, when he was too tired.

She said, "I haven't slept for five days!" She wiped her eyes with her hand. "All I do, all day every day, is go from town, to town, trying to make people vote for me!"

Then the Prime Minister started to cry too. "I've been doing this for five years!" He said, "All I wanted to do was make everything fair!"

Adam took his hand and led him over to the window. "Look," said Adam, "everything IS fair!"

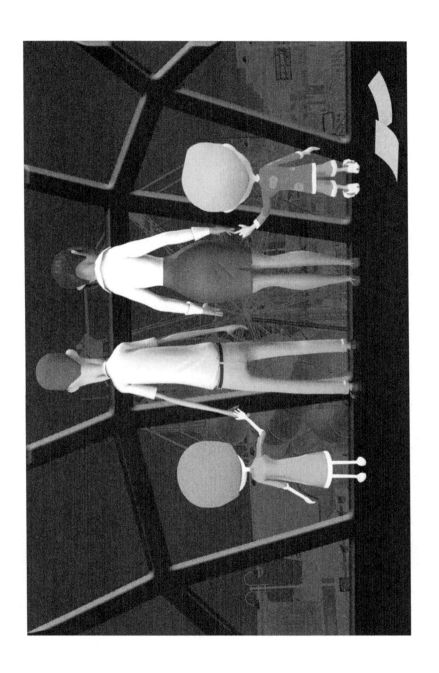

I took the lady's hand, and we went over to stand next to him. I looked out over the town, where the hundreds and thousands of little lights covered the roller-coaster, winding round and round the buildings, and the rides and the stalls, and everything flashed and whirled around below us.

Outside, the news people were flying past in their helicopter, trying to take pictures.

"No," I said, "everything is A FAIR. That's not the same."

Adam and I took the Prime Minister, and the lady who wanted to be Prime Minister to the back, and sat them down. They both curled up and went to sleep.

The problem is that being Prime Minister is a really big job. There's so much to think about that it's too hard for anyone to get everything right.

You also have to keep Acting Normal, and pretending that you can get everything right, even when everyone knows you can't.

And even when you think you've done something really good like turning the whole town into a fair, for the children, and a circus for the grown-ups, there are problems, because nobody can get to school, or get to the shops, or clean up the litter, and there are ghosts in the shopping centre.

It's all a bit crazy, and you would think people would have found a better way to decide things, but they really, really haven't.

All this makes me wonder what I will do when I'm Prime Minister...

CHAPTER 9

While the Prime Minister, and the lady who wanted to be Prime Minister were asleep, my brother sat and read their speeches.

I decided we should probably come down, so I got a piece of paper, and wrote, "Get my Dad," on it and held it up so that the news people in the helicopter could read it.

A few minutes later, the helicopter came back with Dad in the back. I drew him a little picture of the control box and the battery, and he gave me the "thumbs up," signal, which meant he knew what I wanted him to do.

A little while after that, he must have got the wheel connected up because we started moving again.

At the bottom, I could see the news people all crowding round waiting for us. I woke up the Prime Minister, and the lady who wanted to be Prime Minister, and told them it was time to give their speeches.

When the ride stopped and the doors opened, the cameras flashed so brightly, it was hard to see, and while the two grown-ups started to read their speeches out for the news people, Adam and I crept away into the crowd, where Dad was waiting.

The thing is, when Adam was reading the speeches, it was a bit like when he was reading the instructions for the fairs. He didn't exactly know which pages went with which speech, so they might have got what they were saying a bit mixed up.

Still, I don't think anyone will notice if we all just Act Normal...

The end.

Act Normal and read more...

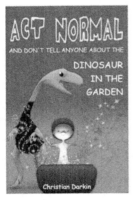